Samuel F. Wight

Adventures in California and Nicaragua, in rhyme

Samuel F. Wight

Adventures in California and Nicaragua, in rhyme

ISBN/EAN: 9783743335400

Manufactured in Europe, USA, Canada, Australia, Japa

Cover: Foto ©Andreas Hilbeck / pixelio.de

Manufactured and distributed by brebook publishing software
(www.brebook.com)

Samuel F. Wight

Adventures in California and Nicaragua, in rhyme

ADVENTURES

IN

California and Nicaragua,

IN RHYME

A TRUTHFUL EPIC:

BY

SAMUEL F. WIGHT

BOSTON:
PRINTED BY ALFRED MUDGE & SON, 34 SCHOOL STREET
1860.

PREFACE.

For the publication of the present volume, no apology is deemed needful, for the reasons that the press is free, and book-reading is not compulsory. The author is not proud of his achievement, nor, on the other hand, does he feel any considerable degree of humility in contemplating it. The latter fact probably arises from a deficiency of judgment.

Of the literary merit of the work, the writer would say but little, trusting that the reader will readily concede to the propriety of so doing. Though written in rhyme, the book contains far "more truth than poetry"; otherwise it would carry but a poor recommendation for veracity.

Begging the pardon of honest readers for what may appear to be a culpable disregard of their good opinion, the author would earnestly solicit the attention of critics, in the reasonable hope, that a class of beings who had the acuteness to discover that Keats and Byron had mistaken their calling, will at once pronounce this work to be the culmination of poetic genius. The narrative is a truthful recital of events in the author's experience.

Part First.

LEAVING HOME.

ADVENTURES

IN

CALIFORNIA AND NICARAGUA.

These rambling lines a truthful story tell,
Of divers haps that to the writer fell,
When from his home, at eighteen years of age,
He wandered forth the war of life to wage,
Friendless and lone, beyond the swelling tide
Whose waters wash Columbia's western side.
For full five years, on California's shore,
Adventurers in search of golden ore
Had gathered fast; a host from ev'ry land,
From Lapland's ice to Afric's burning sand.
From east and west, the old world and the new,
Were gathered there, full many a hardy crew.

In boyish hope kind friends were left behind,
But feelings sad threw shadows o'er my mind.
Bright childhood's home! 't is hard to say adieu.
Sweet scenes of youth! shall ever I review
Thy meadows green, and hills oft wandered o'er;
Or may they glad my vision nevermore?

Ah! soon may drift this body by the strand;
These bones may bleach upon a foreign land.
But, senseless Hope disdained to augur ill,
And won Resolve to pledge a stronger will.

At Gotham town, to sail for Navy Bay,
In waiting, then, the North Star steamer lay.
'T was in July of 'fifty four, we sailed,
'Neath pennon broad that from the mainmast trailed;
And deaf'ning shouts that cheered us on our way,
Soon fainter grew, and distant, died away.
Then down New Jersey's shore swift did we glide,
And safely crossed the Gulf Stream's stormy tide.
Then, sailing south, by Cuba's lovely isle,
The Windward Passage bearing west the while,
Hayti and Jamaica to left appeared,
And southward through Caribbean we steered.

Calm was the sea, beneath a cloudless sky,
And for the palm, with zephyrs did it vie.
Yet, on the way, one incident occurred,
That from repose the calmest bosom stirred.
A fire broke out, deep in the steamer's hold,
And quick aloft the smoke in columns rolled.
The women shrieked,—strong men stood still in fear:
On ocean wide,—no human help was near.
No isle appeared, our sinking hopes to raise,
No friendly ship, to break the ocean maze.
But, Fortune smiled; the fury of the flame
Was soon compelled to yield its lawless claim.

Nine days passed on, then while the morn was gray,
We entered Aspinwall, on Navy Bay.

The railway cars were waiting on the wharf—
One " All aboard," a puff, and we were off.
" Twelve dollars, gents, or tickets for your fare,"
An *" hombre"* cried, with quite a Spanish air.
The heartless mandate made our purses weep,
But, some were short, so grief could not be deep.

To our cold eyes a thousand scenes were new,
And wondrous sights fast crowded into view.
Huge forest kings in stately splendor stood,
That scarce had bowed since God pronounced them good.
Towering palms in noble beauty grew,
' Mid vegetation dense of varied hue,
Whose leaves among, sweet tiny minstrels sang,
In notes of joy that through the forest rang.
Parrots, with knowing looks, were fain to speak,
And nimble apes were playing " hide and seek."

Twice, on that day, the engine left its track,
And twice we toiled to bring the truant back.
But, with the sun, Gorgona passed from sight,
And out we sprang as day dissolved in night.

The air was hot, and being thirsty,—quite,
In search of springs we trod the shades of night;
But sought in vain; no water there was found,
And darkness, thick, was falling fast around.
Yet, spying soon a native with a pail,
We loudly called, " Bring us of Adam's Ale."
" One dime per glass," was said in quick reply.
" What! pay for water? Let us, rather, die."
But nature said, " 'T is money versus life,
So pay the dime, and cease your useless strife."

From early morn till twilight's gentle fall,
Scarce forty miles had passed from Aspinwall,
And now ensconced within a forest deep,
Damp earth a couch,—we laid us down to sleep.

Nature reclined in her dewy repose,
And the murm'ring sound of her breath arose.
The heavy air in languid beauty fell,
And, subtle, crept through forest glade, and dell;
Where, casting down its freight of pearly dew,
Again it rose to roam the forest through;
Singing its songs the sullen trees to cheer;
Waking the leaf by whispers in its ear.

Day rose, and from earth's mantle stole the dew,
And all prepared, in strength and vigor new,
To tread the path through which our journey lay,
For eighteen miles, a rugged, mountain way.
"A mule! A mule!" was soon the only cry;
Yet some preferred to walk; the reason why,
In simple truth is very briefly told:
Within their purses,—light the weight of gold.

A company, myself and other four,
Not cumbered much with surplus weight of ore,
Now jointly hired a driver and his beast,
And from our chattels quickly were released.
Across the mule we strapped a baggage car,
Then onward marched for Bay of Panama.

Wet was the pass, and deep the miry clay;
Fierce from above, down shot the solar ray;

Yet, onward still, the mule and driver went,
Till strength was gone, and respiration spent.
In truth, it seemed the rascal native's aim,
To tire us out, that he might steal the game.
Thus, soon exhausted, comrades lagged behind,
By which all care of baggage they resigned.

Of all our band, five hundred and fifteen,
Scarce more than three were ere together seen.
Each by himself was satisfied to go,
Content was each his own affairs to know.

When scarce was half our tiresome journey o'er,
In haste there met us, twenty-five, or more,
Americans all, who, haggard and pale,
Quick bade us list, and told a fearful tale.
For New York bound, from California, they
Old Panama had left at early day.
But when the pass more lone and darksome grew,
The western waters fading from their view,
A robber band from thicket dense outsprang,
Highwaymen bold, a fierce and bloody gang.
" Your money, boys!   'T is not your lives we ask;
Yet, but resist, and death shall be our task."
Some boldly turned, the cruel foe to fight,
Relief some sought by instantaneous flight.
But, truth to tell, and make the story short,
One man was killed; two runaways were caught.
That vital part, the pocket, was assailed,
And hard earned gold the breath of being bailed.

We journeyed on with watchful eye ahead,
And silent mused on being's brittle thread;

Yet might have moved more cheerfully, and bold;
For blood was not the robbers' aim, but gold.
They lurked not there, in mountain wilds, for fame,
And shooting us, would prove a bootless game.
Full well they knew, that, being outward bound,
Within our purses, little would be found.

Soon passing by the rugged mountain chain,
Whose lofty peaks descend a fertile plain,
With joy we saw, where, conscious in their pride,
The dark blue waves roll o'er the western tide;
And Panama's battlements rose in sight,
Whose giant walls were once the Spaniard's might.

On ev'ry side, 'mid fragrant herbs and flow'rs,
The lime trees crouch, and high the palm tree tow'rs;
While tropic fruits in rich profusion grow,
And bending trees reflect the sunlight's glow.

Around the town extends a fortress wall,
Of ancient look, with portals, massive, tall,
Which soon were passed, and looking down the street,
A large hotel my vision chanced to greet.
On drawing near, " mine host " with features bland,
Sent lackeys out to execute command;
But while his mind he thought a sealed-up book,
Out from his eye, there stole a knavish look.
Yet from his load the mule was quick released,
And on their way went driver and his beast.
As now I sought accommodations meet,
My comrades four came running down the street.
" Our baggage where ? " at once they eager say.
" See yon hotel ? there go without delay."

Another inn soon caught my wand'ring eye,
"City Hotel," whose claims were not passed by.

The weary hours dragged slowly through the night,
But daylight came, at last, and put to flight
The offspring of a gloomy, midnight hour,
And quick dissolved imagination's power.

The noontide came, yet vain did we repine;
Our boat came not, till when at day's decline,
The sun began his golden face to lave,
And hide himself behind the western wave.
Then, in the bay the Uncle Sam appeared,
As swiftly to her anchorage she neared.
But now 't was learned, by some with great dismay,
That ere we left, a dollar each must pay;
For true it was, though seeming very queer:
Upon the strand was no extending pier.
So row-boats small, and oarsmen we must hire,
Of wretches, who, save gold, knew no desire.
We went aboard, but when the list was read.
Thirteen were missed, or, so the purser said.
Some had, perchance, been murdered on the way;
One, sick in town, of yellow fever, lay.

The morning came, and found us on our way,
As, bearing north, we left the spacious bay:
But angry clouds the sky had overcast,
Which gathered thick, and soon were falling fast.
Two days and nights the rain incessant fell,
Which chained us low, like felons in a cell.
The fever, then, his work of death began,
And through the boat a race malignant ran.

So swift and sure the sallow demon's pace,
That while we gazed, each in another's face,
Some victims new he instant marked his own,
By signs that through their changing features shone.
Yet, sailing north, the air became more chill,
And old Disease himself, in turn, grew ill.
But, ere his own, the cruel elf resigned,
Four lives to Death, his partner, he consigned.

Though checked the boat whene'er a life had fled,
No prayer was made, no fun'ral service read.
Each lifeless form, in canvas shroud enrolled,
Was quick consigned to ocean's waters cold.
Then found it there, beneath the dark blue wave,
A resting place, a peaceful, wat'ry grave?
Or did the shark, his hunger to appease,
Voraciously upon each body seize?
Ah! dire the thought that to our minds appealed,
And dread the truth that soon itself revealed;
For, swift the sharks did greedily pursue,
And dart around our steamer as she flew.
Like famished wolves, in greedy haste they moved,
With appetites by taste of food improved.

Time slowly dragged, as on our course we went,
Yet ne'er would thought submit to discontent;
For, on our right, the Rocky Mountain chain
In beauty rose, behind a fertile plain.
Tow'ring peaks with ever-smiling face,
Above the clouds, peered down in lofty grace,
While vapors dense, illumed by sunlight's glow,
Lay on their breasts like shining banks of snow.

Then, farther north, approaching near the coast,
The landscape reared a giant, snow capped host.
Nor could the eye the wat'ry west disdain;
The beautiful on ocean's broad domain.
'T was beautiful to view the fading light,
As lovely day sank in the arms of night;
As Sol reclined in slumber on the deep,
And nature hid her saddened face to weep,—
In ruby light, the day's last sighs exhaust.
His deep'ning hues are soon in darkness lost.
The modest moon, made watcher of the night,
The stars grow bold, and twinkle with delight;
While silv'ry clouds by Zephyrus' breath are driv'n
Like chariots bright, across the arch of heav'n.
Morn comes again, and with her new-born light,
Winged fishes rise, and take their clumsy flight.
Now, mammoth whales in sable mantles shine,
Or sperm whales gray, in sluggish ease recline,—
Such varied scenes relieved full many an hour,
And silence robbed of half its dead'ning pow'r.

From Panama, full thirteen days we sailed,
When El Dorado's shore our vision hailed.
As evening came, we passed old Monterey,
And midnight met in San Francisco Bay,
Where, anchored safe, we passed the silent night,
And with the morning viewed St. Francis' height.

Grand was the scene, as wide our eyes were cast,
Gigantic hills, and dim blue mountains vast
In distance rose, while barren hills of sand,
Composed, entire, the intervening land.
Though looks sublime, all faded nature's dress;
Naught right or left, save dry unfruitfulness;

No pleasing shade, the weary eye gave rest;
No lovely spot, in vegetation blest.
The grand, sublime, lone ruled in proud despair,
For nature, in her beauty, dwelt not there.

Though now from home, six thousand miles, or more,
With just ten dimes remaining of my store,
'T was ne'er in mind to rue a hasty choice,
And thought scarce spoke reflection's sober voice.
But, light of heart, with pockets doubtless lighter,
The siren Hope said, things would soon be brighter.

On Davis' wharf we quickly scrambled out,
To pick up gold like pebble stones,—no doubt.
But vain the hope, the dream of golden weal,
For sterner fact each heart was soon to feel.

Seventy cents was all my money now —
To "make a raise," I truly knew not how;
For lawyers, e'en, though deep and broad of head,
Were digging sand to earn their daily bread.
But, plodding on, my fortune 't was to meet
A man in search for binders of his wheat.
Employed were three, yet other three he sought;
So with him I engaged, with scarce the thought,
That binding wheat was anything but play,
For which was promised, three dollars per day.
Complying now with poverty's behest,
My better coat (two only were possessed)
Was quickly sold to a miserly Jew,
For which, the sum received, was dollars two.
Then sailing o'er the waves ten miles away,
To San Antoine, beyond the spreading Bay,

The stage I took (haply the fare was down)
To Evans' Ranch, by San Lorenzo's town.

The morning came; all bravely took the field,
But ere an hour, my strength began to yield;
So from the labor turning with dismay,
The ranch I left beside the noon of day.

Twelve miles were passed, then Union City came;
A petty vill, called city by misname.
One flour mill, six dwellings, and two inns,
Three gaming shops, with liquor and ten-pins.

Though shades of night had gathered thick around,
No sheltered nook for lodging place was found.
The "houses," true, presented ample fare,
But money, then, was what 't were hard to spare.
Yet soon, by chance, in distance came to view,
A row of pig-pens thatched with wheat straw new.
No human form was near, nor spoke the breeze
In aught save grunts that told of swinish ease.
So, climbing up, I made a dreary bed,
By spreading sheaves to serve in blankets stead.

Fancy portrayed me 'alone to my glory,'
But, soon came a noise from the basement story.
Pigs would be pigs, and so they squealed and fought,
Till, by the morn, a flag of truce was brought.
It seemed as though, more hoggish than the rest,
One had resolved to have full half the nest.
Misguided pig! How much like human kind,
To pamper self, and leave the world behind!

3

Monopoly, no creature will allow,
Though man, or brute, the finale is a row.

As sombre night must always yield to day,
And darkness wane, dissolved by morning's ray,
So there, at last, the shadows of the night
In silence sped, before approaching light.
Then creeping down, I took a morning stroll,
And for a breakfast, ate a baker's roll.
Then, turning northward, left the town behind,
As naught was there to satisfy my mind.

At San Lorenzo, fourteen miles away,
A stream I crossed, and met the noon of day.
Chanced also, there, a husbandman to meet,
And once again engaged for binding wheat.

Thus spoke the man: "A day and half a day,
The closing of the week, you'll work to pay
The cost of board till Monday's sun draws nigh,
For here in California, 'grub' is high.
Two dollars fifty cents, each working day,
Shall pay your labor while you choose to stay."

When Monday's sun raised nature's sable veil,
To work I went, but strength began to fail.
Then two day's strife with fate passed by in vain,
And work was left for wandering again.
With morning's light I passed by San Antoine,
To Contra Costa, best as Oakland known.
Crossed then the bay, to roam Francisco o'er,
Though fruitlessly as on the week before.

The morning came, but brought no cheer for me ;
Misfortune's face 't was yet my lot to see.
Hope bravely spoke, but Thought was very sad,
For, one lone dime was all the coin I had.

Travelling west, Dolores came to view,
But, passing on, her walls as quickly flew.

The morning fled ; the noontide came and went,
But, reckless grown, Thought cared not to lament ;
And when from town full fifteen miles had passed,
Employ I found upon a grain field vast ;
Through nine days toiled, then back again returned.
And, over Sabbath, in the town sojourned.
Then crossing o'er, again, Francisco Bay,
Viewed San Lorenzo ere the dusk of day.

True to itself, consistent as of late,
Still, evil shone my luckless star of fate.
My funds again were running very low,
And yet, "to raise the dust," there was "no show."
So, hasting back, two rolls I bought to eat,
Then fell asleep beside a stack of wheat.
At morn, arose, with strength and vigor new,
And soon engaged to help an old French Jew.

On horse-back he had ridden, rather flown,
Two miles, post haste, from village San Anoine.
"A mob," said he, "just now I've been among ;
For stealing cows, two Frenchmen have been hung."
Two butchers, they, I from his story learned,
Who, lawlessly, had thus their "*carne*" earned.

But, with intent to right the suffered wrong,
The "Redwood Boys" came down a hundred strong.
The wretched men were sentenced to be hung,
Though loud they plead, and to existence clung.
But, ere was fixed the life destroying tie,
A woman came, who thus began to cry :
"Here's eighteen thousand, all in solid gold,
But from these men release your murd'rous hold."
"Ah! woman, no!" the "Redwood Boys" replied ;
'Mid earth and sky,—then quick the felons died.

A look there was about the old man's eye,
An evil glance that did not satisfy ;
But, times were hard, and folly 't were to choose ;
So work I must, though gladly would refuse.

Six weeks were passed, among a medley gang,
'Mid varied languages, and mongrel twang.
Thirty-five men,—whom ev'ry land could boast,
A multiform, heterogeneous host.
Grave Spaniards, English, one East Indiaman,
Gay men of France, and French Canadian,
Bold Irishmen, with Dutch, both high and low,
Californians, and sons of Mexico,
Chilese polite, and brave Norwegians bland,
With five to represent our own free land.

Alone, one day, dull valley scenes to change,
I wandered off upon a mountain range.
Though nature seemed her faded dress to wail,
September glanced in smiles athwart the vale.
But lo! three miles in distance from the plain,
'Neath frowning clouds, was thick the falling rain ;
And "mountain boys" made question as we met :
"Upon the plains, the weather, is it wet?"

"Far from it, boys; the plains are very dry,
And bright the sun smiles from a cloudless sky."
With some surprise at once their voices raise:
"Ah! say you so? This storm has raged three days."

A man ere long at Oakland town was hung;
Horse-stealing was the crime for which he swung.—
In county jail, where, by the law confined,
The wretched man protection thought to find;
But, vain the hope; scarce in his lonely cell,
Aloud is heard the mob's terrific yell.
They draw him forth,—nor heed his thrilling cries.—
Then,—'mid the branches of an oak,—he dies.

A brandy-loving Frenchman was our cook,
Who for his cup, the kitchen oft forsook.
More clear to show how far from right he'd swerve,
An anecdote, itself, shall briefly serve.
Of hungry dogs a dozen, more or less,
The Frenchman's pride, 't was, solely to possess.
As from the field one day, the house we neared,
No cook, nor dogs, with wonted smiles appeared.
But, walking in, the reason soon was shown:
Although the board beneath its weight might groan,
No cook appeared; but, all the dogs were there,
And, on the table, two found dainty fare.
The larger one, for appetite's relief,
Was finishing his dish of roasted beef.
One shaggy head was in a dish of soup,
While both were scat'ring sundries to the group.

Once more, alas! Misfortune's hated form
Stole o'er my path,—within her hand a storm.

One morning bright, our thresher's mighty pow'r
Had scarce begun the wheat sheaves to devour,
When, lo! a man by ev'ry one unknown,
Took all our horses down to San Antoine.
The sheriff 't was, as soon he bade us know,
And quick complied, when told his writ to show.
Machine and other implements were seized,
That creditors' cries might be appeased.
So naught was left, the laborers to pay,
And, penniless, full many went away.
The wheat remained, but that gave no relief,
For, of it all, the Jew ne'er owned a sheaf.
In short to tell, five dollars some received,
While many men without a penny grieved.
What course to take, seemed difficult of choice,
But, as we left, a man from Illinois,
Who from the Plains arrived three weeks before,
And for the Jew had worked a week, or more,
Quick made approach, and thus his words addressed:
"Five dollars, you, of twelve am I possessed.
What say you, shall we put it all together,
And seek the mines upon the river Feather?
The rains come soon, and there, as I am told,
Are diggings new, and very rich in gold.
We're just in time, before the rain sets in,
To stake out claims, all ready to begin."

In company, we walked without delay,
To San Antoine, and crossed Francisco Bay.
Six men-of-war were lying off the town,
Which, as we learned, had from the north come down.
An Anglo French, or Allied fleet they formed,
Which had of late a Russian fortress stormed;

But, Sitka's guns were so expertly aimed,
Repulsed were they with vessels sadly maimed.
Then, sailing south, they captured on the way,
A merchant ship, and made Francisco Bay.

The boat at four, for Sacramento sailed,
And, high in hope, as better fortune failed,
The fare we paid, five dollars for the deck,
Which well nigh proved our scanty fortune's wreck.

Slow was the boat, and chill the air of night,
As, on the deck, we watched for morning's light.
'Till midnight, near, we ploughed a wat'ry field,
When bleak Benicia's dreary face revealed.
We briefly paused, then with the smiling moon,
Crossed o'er the face of lovely Suisun.

With break of day the city came in sight,
And on the levee all did safe alight.
Though seven times twenty miles above the bay,
The waters here, the changing tides display;
And barges, ranged along the river's brink,
With tide arise, and with its ebbing sink.

Wide spreads the plain on which the city stands,
While, all around, lie fertile garden lands.
The American forms the northern bound;
The Sacramento walls the west around:
Then south and east, are spread to close the scene,
With valleys Sacramento, and Joaquin.

Now leaving town for Marysville intent,
By some mistake, our steps from J street bent.
Old Sutter's Fort we left upon the right,
But soon observed the river fade from sight;
So questioning an "*hombre*," passing by,
Our anxious query met this grave reply:
" In truth, my friends, you've gone three miles astray;
This road, to Prairie City leads the way;
Turn right about, if Marysville you'd find;
From Sacramento, north, your steps must wind;
Lisle's Bridge you'll cross, the river trail then take,
And in two days the journey you can make."

Travelling back, we took the proper way,
Disheartened, near, by reason of delay;
The toll-bridge crossed, four bits were forced to pay,
And tow'rd the north, bore rapid on our way;
Travelling o'er, in full, six prairie miles,
Before the sun looked down in noonday smiles.
Naught easier than walking would we ask;
But carrying packs was another task.

A loaded team soon passing chanced to be,
When looking up, companion said to me:
" We'll hail the man, and of him then inquire,
If, to his knowledge, any wish to hire.
Of cash, you know, we've but a scanty store,
And Marysville lies sixty miles before."

The man, by chance, a tradesman wished to hire;
" To build a barn," said he, " is my desire."
A carpenter, companion was by trade.
And, on the spot, a contract quick was made.

As on I went, with resolution new,
Determined still, the journey to pursue,
Aloud the teamster called, and to me said,
"The miner's life is one that I have led.
Be now advised; let my experience be
A warning voice, and satisfying plea.
This oft is called a God-forsaken land,
But, truly so, the prostituted hand
That delves in earth, intent to rob the soil
Of wealth, the fit reward of honest toil.
And, furthermore, it is not time to mine;
Where one finds gold, lank Poverty finds nine.
Until the rains, as doubtless you've been told,
There's scarce a 'show' for washing out your gold.
Rejoices yet, September in her prime;
Look not for gold in this ungen'rous clime,
Till winter's blast, down yonder mountain's side,
From snowy peaks, shall roll a fleecy tide."

Now turning back, I clambered on the load,
And with them back to Sacramento rode;
Then left my friend, nor saw his face again,
Though often sought,—the search was always vain.

Three men, by chance appeared, rough farmers all,
Who owned, in company, a sail-boat small;
And on their ranch, a helping hand to lend,
I soon engaged, the river to descend.
'T was fifty miles, or more, below the town,
And in the sail-boat all must needs go down.

Upon the morrow, ere the rising sun,
Our downward trip was merrily begun.

4

The morn was bright, and soft the whisp'ring breeze
Came sporting through the overhanging trees.
Her brightest smile, sweet nature cheerful gave,
And brightly smiled, in turn, the gentle wave.
The winding stream in sparkling beauty ran,
While sycamores bent gracefully to fan
Her lovely form, whene'er the king of day
Should grasp again, the reins of wonted sway.

Day at his closing, ushered in the night,
When Sol resigned to Luna's milder light;
And boist'rous winds, though hiding through the day,
At night sprang out, with mother Earth to play.
The tall trees rocked, the giddy waters danced,
While o'er the spray, our boat, a charger, pranced.

Day crept, once more, above the eastern plain,
And by his light, our journey did we gain.
Twelve miles above, the stream divides in two;
Old River, one, the other, Steamboat Slough.
Three miles below, their hands again unite,
And soon the tides, with outstretched arms, invite
Those pure mountain waters, their haste to delay,
And make them a home in the wide-spreading bay.

For full five weeks, in that secluded place,
Each day, appeared Old River's smiling face.
A schooner, then, one morn, to land drew nigh,
Whose master chanced a freight of wood to buy;
And on her deck, a passage free I found,
To San Francisco, whither she was bound.
Bianca was the name she truly bore,
But sad mishap had christened something more.

At sundry times, her widely sweeping boom
Had hurled a man from deck to wat'ry doom;
And scarce had yet three days and nights gone by,
Since, with her freight, she sank by daylight's eye.
Bloody Bianca, now her fated name,
Perpetual spoke her sanguinary fame.

Two days and nights, the vessel ploughed her way,
Then, on the third, at San Francisco lay.

The " People's Line " of river opposition,
Had brought about a wonderful transition:
Two bits, the fare, was so extremely low,
That back again I quickly thought to go.

At one o'clock, arrived, all went ashore,
And Sacramento town was viewed once more.

Now, back and forth, five trips in all I made,
Then o'er one week in Sacramento staid.
The end in view, thus going to and fro,
An explanation brief, will clearly show:
Ere from my home, the land of gold was sought,
Two years, 'mid busy wheels, my hands had wrought.
'T was hope held out, in shops, employ to find,
Than tilling earth, more pleasing to my mind.

Again, alas! my purse was nearly drained,
Of thirty-five, no dollar there remained.
Yet, still resolved the miner's life to try,
With spirits good, though not exceeding high,
My chattels all, in one small pack I rolled,
And lone, on foot, looked toward the land of gold.

The self-same road, began to travel o'er,
As with my comrade just six weeks before.
Though frowning clouds had gathered thick o'erhead,
With hasting steps, and silently, I sped;
But soon the rain descended thick and fast,
The torrent roared; relentless blew the blast;
And earth beneath, still soft, and softer grew,
Till weights of clay adhered to either shoe.

In grand array the distant mountains rose,
With lofty peaks capped by eternal snows;
And on the left, the Sutter Buttes appeared,
Whose lofty heads in grandeur bold upreared.

The noonday came; a tavern chanced to be
Upon the right, but spoke no hope to me.
Hungry and cold, I passed it with a sigh,
For twenty cents would not suffice to buy.

Near daylight's close, a village came to view,
And hasting on, though scarce a reason knew,
I entered Nicholaus on the Feather,
Or, on the Bear, as both streams come together.
Though small the village was, two inns were there,
For through its center passed a thoroughfare.
From Sacramento thirty miles away,
It served to close the journey of a day.

Pale Hunger chid, yet by the town I passed,
For, of "two bits," dared not to spend the last.
But, walking on, a man in passing said,
" If work you seek go on two miles ahead;

For, there you'll find a man who seeks a hand
To fell the oaks that grow upon his land."

The sun went down, and faster fell the rain,
Till one broad lake, seemed that wide-spreading plain.
Night hurried on; her shades she threw around,
When howled the wolf with distant, dismal sound.

No house appeared; no light shone out before,
Yet, " sure," thought I, " two miles are travelled o'er."
The darkness thick revealed no place of rest,
Not e'en of distant woodland, to suggest
The spreading arms of some half-conscious oak,
Whose shelt'ring pow'r might ward the tempest's stroke.

The thought soon came: 'T were wiser, now, to turn,
Than longer strive against a fate so stern,
But, vain attempt! alas! no trail was there,
The path to point; returning steps to bear.

Now, wretched owls their hideous notes prolong,
And other tribes chime in with dismal song;
But from their din a useful hint I take,
And loudly sing for failing nature's sake.
The notes thus raised, which might have shamed the owls,
Brought no response, save distant, wolfish howls.
In vain, sharp vision strove to pierce the night,
With hope to catch some distant, friendly light.
My weary limbs would fain their task forsake,
And soon, it seemed, grim Death the spell must break.

At midnight, near, the storm his fury ceased,
And scatt'ring clouds the prisoned stars released.

Old Darkness still upheld his gloomy sway,
But two black lines soon faintly bade me stay.
And, starlight dim by feeble rays displayed,
Where two cross roads four equal angles made.
"But still," said Thought, "the danger is not o'er;
The way to town, which is it of the four?"
North, south, east, west were quite alike to me,
And each, in turn, the right way seemed to be.
But soon, a plan came haply into mind:
"If one be right, that way I yet may find."
Reflecting, then, that early in the night,
The chilling tide had drifted from the right,
That road I sought which turned the blast around,
And quite reversed the howling tempest's sound.
Then hasting on, a distant light appeared,
And in an hour, the town I gladly neared.
One public house was still all brightly lit,
For, near the bar did eager gamblers sit.
Red-hot the stove, for, with a frequent lunch,
The players cried, " Bring us hot whiskey punch!"
Behind his bar the landlord waiting stood,
To measure out his gin and brandy, good.

'T was one o'clock; full fifteen hours had fled,
With naught of rest, nor yet the taste of bread.
From head to foot, all covered o'er with mire,
For full an hour, I sat beside the fire;
Then with the hope, worse evil to prevent,
For whiskey punch my last two bits were spent.
'T was habit new, and drinking from the brim,
My head grew light, and eyesight somewhat dim.
I told the landlord how the night had flown,
But did not make my destitution known.

For supper called, but, little cared for bread,
As whiskey punch had sadly turned my head.

One room contained, all lying on the floor,
Of Chinamen, no less than twenty-four,
Who, in their native costume fully dressed,
Profoundly slept like pigs within a nest.

At two o'clock the gamblers ceased their game,
With sundry oaths, too monstrous here to name.
Then, calling for lodging, in sleep profound,
My weary frame found rest, and care was drowned.

Dawn's feebler light had strengthened into day,
Ere from my bedside, Morpheus stole away.

The house I left, intent to take a view,
And plan, meanwhile, some project to pursue,
But scarce had passed the threshold of the door,
When quickly running from a grocery store,
A drover came, whose home was Suisun,
And fast began to talk, as for a boon.
A drove of pigs had he, but in the night
His boy grew ill, which left him in a plight.
"For two dollars a day, and board," said he,
"Will you help drive these pigs to Cherokee?"
To pay, advance, whate'er my bill should need,
Without delay he readily agreed.
Though far or near, I little cared to know,
And quick engaged upon the trip to go;
But soon he said, "'T is seventy miles away,
Of which we hope to make fifteen per day."
His partner was a man from Tennessee,
Pike County man, himself professed to be.

Two teams had they, small bags of flour, the freight,
Two horses, one, the other, oxen eight.
Beside the town encamping for the night,
A fire we made to put the wolves to flight.
Then hasting on with morning's earliest ray,
The sunset found us twenty miles away.
The road we travelled, I remembered well: —
'T was where the owls had thought to scream my knell.
Five miles from town, the two cross roads we found;
Where cruel Night had dragged me round and round.
Nor was it strange no light should there appear,
And naught of sound had wafted to my ear.
Ten miles were passed, before a cabin rose,
Or e'en a tree, its shade to interpose.

At noon of day, we crossed the river Bear,
And travelled on till day began to wear.
When, o'er Dry Creek, upon the farther side,
Good camping ground, with water, pure, was spied.
A stove we had, by which to bake our bread,
And blazing camp-fires served in candles' stead.
The pigs we drove, for safety, near the fire,
As hungry wolves were howling their desire.

Sixty-two miles fled southward; then at eve,
Near French Corral, day claimed a fourth reprieve;
And o'er our forest camp, night swiftly sped,
Till, with the dawn, her waning form waxed red.
We passed the hours, by day's command set free,
And with him viewed the town of Cherokee.

The pigs we left, a fat, contented band,
To roam the hills, and graze the mountain land;

Then left for Marysville at break of day,
Consuming thirty hours upon the way.
At Suisun, a ranch the men possessed.
Till, to their thoughts, reflection did suggest,
That near the mines, if no ill luck befel,
A tannery would pay extremely well.
Then packing up, they started with a will,
Leaving their "goods" to come by Marysville.

Wandering Impulse, now as oft before,
Blind, senseless pilot, ran my bark ashore.
With strong desire, Nevada town to see,
Though to the thought, good sense would not agree,
Full forty miles, on foot, I did pursue,
Elate with hope of some adventure new.
The Twelve Mile House, I passed at eventide,
And soon prepared, till morning to abide;
A camp-fire, made, and in that forest lone,
In silence, laid my head upon a stone;
Yet oft within those chilly hours did wake,
With trembling hands, the dying coals to rake;
Then leaving camp ere yet the sun arose,
Nevada came, before the day's repose.
Small mining towns, upon the way were passed,
With which, young Rough and Ready may be classed.
Grass Valley, too, seemed quite a thriving town,
Where many a hill, for gold had melted down;
Then four miles on, low in a deep ravine,
Nevada lay, high mountain lands between.

To mine for gold, I vainly there essayed,
And gamblers, then, monopolized the trade.

5

The public houses scarcely could contain
The miners, woe-begone for lack of rain.
So, with the morn, I left for Marysville,
Retraced the way with hasting steps, until
Full thirty-six, of forty miles were gained,
When darkness thick, my weary feet arraigned.
The night I passed, upon a stack of hay,
But ere the morn, perceived with great dismay,
That from thick clouds the scatt'ring rain drops fell,
Which soon increased; in torrents came, pell-mell.
Full dire the thought of want and added woe,
Yet sadly on, with silent step I go;
And, reaching town, encased in mud and mire,
Soon dry my clothes beside a bar-room fire.

Four frosty nights in chill December's reign,
Passed hopelessly, upon the open plain.
Four days in fruitless rambling there I spent,
Then had for consolation,—not one cent.
Wandering off, scarce knowing what to do,
Six miles, or more, from town, I chanced to view
The old Missourian's partner, on his way
To Cherokee Ranch, with two loads of hay.
Their freight had not at Marysville arrived,
But, hay to get, for carting, they'd contrived.
"Missouri," then had left to see a friend,
Who had engaged some weary pigs to tend,
Which had been left, their vigor to renew,
That, in due time, the trip they might pursue.

A teamster, who, near Marysville was hired,
Had homesick grown, and to return, desired.

Him I relieved for stipulated pay,
Of grub, or food, and two dollars a day.
Four days and nights the journey yet required,
For various haps upon the way transpired.
As, for an instance, when we rose one morn,
To speed our way,—the oxen all were gone;
But, searching round, we found them on a hill,
Six miles behind, going back to Marysville.
Another hap then caused us some delay,
One wagon broke,—down came a load of hay.
At last, arrived, we found "Missouri" there,
Impatient waiting, almost in despair.

To Minnesota, then, we drove the swine,
Full forty miles in a northerly line.
O'er Backbone Bridge, by Grisly Cañon went,
And passed the night, ensconced in old Snow Tent.
From Orleans Flat, by Concord Bar we passed
O'er Yuba's branch, and stood again at last,
Exhausted, all, on Minnesota's height,
The second day, before the fall of night.
'T were well to stay, and though digress too far,
Tell how those pigs went down o'er Concord Bar.
But all whose steps through that ravine have led,
Know well how deep the Yuba cuts her bed.
And all whose way there never chanced to wend,
Would, at the best, but faintly comprehend.
Suffice to say, that save the weary plod
Of patient mules, no burdened beast ere trod
Those fearful heights, which, in their bold ascent,
Deep chasms form, as though the earth were rent.

The pigs were sold, and being once more free,
Reflection's voice her words addressed to me:

"In all its modes, gold digging you have seen;
You're now prepared to judge, those modes between.
If now, indeed, the miner's lot you choose,
'Pitch in' you must; hard labor not refuse.
Here's quartz-rock grinding, flaming, panning,
Tunneling, rocking, and river damming,
Hydraulic pipes, much used for gully sinking,
And other ways, all worth attentive thinking."
But miners, there, in number many a score,
Gray-headed, some, not turned of twenty-four,
One story, all, in mournful accent told,
"If health you value, never dig for gold."

Twelve dollars, now, my fortune all, embraced,
And toward the south, my steps again I traced.
By three days' light, walked seventy miles and five,
And did, with dusk, at Marysville arrive;
Then at the dawning of another day,
Left Marysville for San Francisco Bay.

As oft before, a week now passed in vain,
When sad to tell, "dead broke" was I again.
For Petaloma then, by sloop set sail,
To load with wood, if other freight should fail.
Before we left, a storm convulsed the bay,
And, off Red Rock, the sloop was forced to lay.
That tempest night can ne'er from mem'ry fade,
For, all the pow'rs of nature seemed arrayed,
To roll the hostile waters of the bay,
Upon the land, their empire to display.
'T was old December in a passion wrought;
To lengthen out his cheerless days he sought;
But, 'mid the night, the hopeful infant year,
Did suddenly in Janus' arms appear.

December raved, and stirred the tempest's pow'r;
But all in vain, for Janus ruled the hour.
Cold shrivelled limbs, and age's falt'ring pace,
Were ill a match for New Year's youthful grace.

The captain's voice we often heard that night:
Ho! Boys! On deck, and make her anchor right!
High on the billows' crest, our boat was thrown,
Then, deep engulphed, anon her sides did groan.
But scarce heard we, the tempest's angry sound,
For table, stove, and chairs were dancing round.

Our sails we set, with daylight's first display.
And Petaloma viewed, at close of day.
The stream we sailed, which bears the city's name,
Supports upon its banks, all kinds of game;
And, as a sportsman, captain proved to be,
He quick gave chase, whene'er we chanced to see
An antelope, but ne'er would touch his gun,
For turkey-buzzard, goose, or pelican.

A freight of wood, near forty cords, we took,
Then to the breeze, our spreading canvas shook;
At San Francisco soon discharged the wood,
And in two days, toward Sacramento stood.
The storm that raged so fierce, on New Year's night,
Had left to the city, tokens of might.
Whole roofs were blown, church spires came tumbling down.
And houses fell, in many parts of town.
One vessel sank, while wrecked were many more,
That by the surf were dashed upon the shore.

One hundred miles above, on island lone,
A ranch there was, the captain called his own;

On which, to toil, I now engaged to go;
To clear up the land with a grubbing hoe,
So left the sloop, when forty miles away,
And twenty walked, by light, the self-same day.
Then passed the night, the river's bank beside,
Where, for a pillow, mining boots provide.

Next day, arriving opposite the farm,
I called aloud, the household to alarm,
When slowly came its only tenant out,
And to my call responded with a shout.
Then o'er the stream, he paddled in a boat,
And eager read a "line" which captain wrote,
Then quickly asked, "Which of the week is this?"
"Why! Saturday, unless I'm quite amiss."
"Zounds! I've been keeping Sunday," quick he cried,
With mouth agape, and eye-balls rolling wide.

In grubbing roots, two weary weeks were spent,
But, with such life, 'twas hard to feel content.
The Chills and Fever, also, lent their aid,
To shake my resolution, and persuade
A hesitating mind to delve no more,
As Fortune had some better fate in store.
The ranch I left, and walked without delay,
Toward Sacramento, eighteen miles away;
And, reaching town just in the edge of night,
Upon a woodpile, passed the chilly night.
Now four months' work at gardening, I found,
Upon a ranch within the city's bound.
'Twas near the dike, or levee's north extreme,
Beside the bank where sister waters seem
In haste to join, ere nature gives command,
Their brother Sacramento, heart and hand.

Though in that vale the snow flakes never fall,
The distant mountains, hoary giants, all,
Lift up their heads against a sunlit-sky,
In regions where eternal snow-banks lie.

Two months passed on, with little to excite,
Save bank suspensions, then at zenith height.
Kern River humbug, too, its work began,
Of arming dupes, with pickaxe, spade, and pan.

Some Digger Indians from the north came down,
And made their camp just three half miles from town;
And often, there, when free from work at night,
The boys clubbed round to see them dance, and fight.
Their custom was, by day to cross the stream,
And scour the swamps where berries always teem;
By daylight pick, at evening go and sell,
Buy whiskey, drink, then gamble, fight, and yell.
But shrewder, they, than many of our race;
The weaker sex found in their hearts a place.
Soda they brought, and very plain the cause:
'T was this, they knew, would pacify the squaws,
Good natured things, who'd drag them to the tent,
When strength was gone, and animation spent.

Two farms, there were, that bordered side by side,
On each of which, two months I did reside.
A man from New Orleans, one owner was,
Who, many lawsuits had, with no just cause.
Now on his claim, a house or hovel stood,
Not very large, by Dutchmen built, of wood.
His men one morn he called together, three,
And thus began to issue his decree:

"See yonder house that rises on my land?
Go tear it down! no longer shall it stand."
We knew not, then, a bitter quarrel raged,
Or that a warfare, legal, had been waged,
In which, his suit the Southron, action having lost,
Was forced to pay a heavy bill of cost.
So off we went, with crowbar, axe, and shovel,
And tore away aforesaid Dutchmen's hovel.
But, when complete, and rubbish packed away,
The sheriff came, and this was pleased to say:
"Step in this carriage, now, sirs, if you please,
The cries of broken law you must appease.
Upon the case 't were useless to enlarge,
"Malicious Mischief," doubtless, is the charge.
My writ is here, by which you'll please to see,
Its plain instructions with my acts agree."
The Southerner, ringleader in the play,
Was on the list, and taken on our way.
The cost and twenty dollars, each was fined,
But Southron paid, and we felt quite resigned.
Yet, cool Reflection spoke in tones not sweet,
True names we'd given, honest, not discreet.
Crime's record, thus, our names must ever bear,
Grave dereliction ever to declare.
'T is pleasing, oft, one's name in print to see,
But so, to us, it did not prove to be,
When, plain in type, on the following day,
"Recorder's Court" made such a free display.

The harvest season now came on again,
And gardening was left, for binding grain.
For four day's work, twelve dollars was the pay,
When, wearied quite, I started for the bay.

O'er one day, then, in San Francisco staid,
And on the next, returning passage made.
To Stockton, then, on foot decide to go,
Full fifty miles from city Sacramento.
But, clothes and blankets forming quite a store,
With divers books, in number near a score,
A pack I took, and left in town, the rest,
With wise intent, of burden to divest.

The city passed, and as the twilight neared,
A wayside inn, the Twelve Mile House, appeared.

When morning came, I went not on my way,
But with the landlord, there agreed to stay;
Upon his ranch six working days then spent,
And back again to Sacramento went.
To get my pack, then quickly did repair,
But, when arrived,—alas! no inn was there.
Of all, so late those furnished walls contained,
A mass of ashes, now, alone remained.
Two nights before, when darkness hung around,
The house was burned, with contents, to the ground.
Stern was the truth, though easy to discover:
No one who lost could ere a cent recover.
Though sad the loss, 't were useless now to mourn;
' What could not be prevented must be borne.'

To Stockton, now, by stage, direct I go,
From which, for good, no consequences flow.
The San Joaquin, by steam I did descend
To San Francisco, hoping there to mend
My shattered fortunes, but no longer stay,
Than till the time of harvest passed away.
6

Then leave a land, where fourteen months had flown,
Within whose days, no rest my feet had known.
So crossing south, o'er San Francisco Bay,
Three months I spent near Mission San Jose.
A farewell, then, to Sacramento paid,
And for a homeward trip arrangements made.

Part Second.

RETURNING HOME.

'T was now October; fifteen months had rolled,
Since, high in hope, my home I left for gold.
The bright day dreams of youth's untutored mind,
Had disappeared and left a void behind.
The glit'tring lines that Fancy's hand had traced
Upon life's title page, had Truth erased;
When flashed the thought: Life's romance is a dream,
From which the world's cold hands awake, redeem.

One fact, in brief, for justice must be told:
California's soil was rich in gold;
And that amount, though needless here to say,
Scarce was less when the writer came away.

In action, then, two steamship lines there were,
So to my mind the question did occur:
"Which of the two does prudence bid me take;
By Panama, or Nicaragua's lake?"
Some evil star had seemed my fate to rule,
Control my steps, and turn to ridicule
All wiser thought, when wisdom dared suggest
A wiser plan, or to my own protest.
Adventures new, a change would bring, no doubt:
This thought pronounced for Nicaragua's route.

In civil war poor Nicaragua, now
Lay low engulfed; and he upon whose brow
A zealous world have deeply fixed the brand
Of "fillibuster," there held high command;

In defence of the right, the people's voice,
Commander-in-chief by popular choice.
For thirty years, while Faction's cruel hand
Had bathed in blood the face of that fair land,
Her restless sons with native thirst for strife,
Scarce e'er had sheathed the sanguinary knife.
Revolution, in the cycle of crime,
Had quite out-rolled the yearly orb of time.
Nor were her laws in Order's transient reign,
But iron links in grim Oppression's chain,
With which, in turn, each tyrant sought to bind
The rising thought, that moved the common mind.
The wealthy few, sole power had long possessed,
And, consequent, the masses were oppressed,
Who, in their turn, to native impulse true,
In strife engaged, though why they scarcely knew.
They felt the weight of Persecution's heel,
And Spanish impulse bade them grasp the steel.
But time moved on, and with his steady pace,
As surely moved the Spanish Indian race.
Some feeble rays of Freedom's rising sun,
In that benighted land, had now begun
To pierce their gloom, and rouse the dormant life
Of intellect, to arm in noble strife.
Two castes there were, from which two bands had sprung,
And to its own, tenaciously each clung.
The Liberals, with Indian blood allied,
Were popular, and struggled to provide
Their blood-stained land with democratic laws;
To fix on firmer base, the people's cause.
Against these plans, with wise prevision laid,
The wealthy class in hostile force arrayed.

Though fallen sons of old Castilian race,
Their Spanish pride still held its ancient place.
But recently, their selfish plans had failed,
And, for a time, fair Freedom's cause prevailed.
Yet ever to their restless natures true,
The Serviles raised Rebellion's flag anew.
The principle they had so late professed,
That popular rule were always the best,
With perfidy they quickly now forsook,
Plebean rule, too proud were they to brook.

The war waged fierce, but on the battle field,
The Liberals, at last, were forced to yield.
Castillion fled; the Serviles ruled the day,
Assumed to legislate, held wanton sway.
The fierce Chamorro, by his rebel band,
Was then declared chief ruler of the land.

Liberals, all, assembled round their chief,
And quick devised a plan to bring relief.
As skillful, brave, and to adventure prone,
Already, well, was William Walker known.
To San Francisco he had late returned,
From Mexico with reputation earned
In reckless warfare on Sonora's plain,
With purpose, fell, a foothold there to gain.
His willing hand the Liberals invite,
Their cause to aid, their enemies to fight.
So in the month of May, in fifty-five.
A little band, but fifty, did arrive
On Nicaragua's soil at San Juan,
With Grey-eyed William leading up the van.

He went, 't is true, with more of haste than grace,
With terms arranged as lawyers take a case
Of client poor, who has no means to pay,
Unless, in common phrase, he "gains the day."
"Our cause is just," the vanquished party said,
"But Might slew Right, and reigns in Justice's stead.
The realm is ours; if we possession gain,
Your pay shall be a slice of the domain."
But ere that band had crossed the ocean spray,
In death's cold arms the brave Castillion lay.
Chamorro, also, died,—that leader base,
And brave Corral was chosen in his place.

Infused anew with patriotic ardor,
The Liberals took Leon, and Grenada,
Held Virgin Bay, with San Juan del Sur,
In which position, now, the parties were.

The "fillibuster fever" then held sway,
From Klamath's mouth, to San Diego Bay.
Misfortune's offspring, men of ev'ry grade,
Pickpockets, thieves, and rogues of varied shade,
From hill and dale, in haste were drawing near,
In Nicaragua's cause to volunteer.
As now the hawk had on his victim pounced,
Our government with righteous zeal, pronounced
The game opposed to treaty stipulation,
And deep disgrace to any Christian nation.

The Uncle Sam had long since been removed
From Panama, which route had clearly proved,
A private scheme of selfish competition,
Though loud proclaimed as " People's Opposition."

While on her last, from Nicaragua made,
A deadly scourge, its frightful game had played. .
The Cholera, old Death's obedient slave,
Had sunk two hundred men beneath the wave;
And "Charnel Ship," though fitting appellation,
Was not so good a standing commendation.
Yet, "swept and garnished" all, her plague-stained walls,
The dismal fact no more the mind appalls.
So, high to mast-head quick her flag she ran,
And advertised, "New York, by San Juan."

The day arrived, and dense the motley gang
That round the steamer at her wharf did hang.
Yet, all unheeded came the hour, and went;
Her pier to leave, the boat showed no intent.
But plain the cause, though not a word was told;
The would-be soldiers, lacked the weight of gold,
And consequently, on the wharf must stay,
Till Parker French should come, their fare to pay.

The marshal and his gang did soon arrive,
The boat to search, with purpose hence to drive
All vagabonds, and men of evil eye,
Who had no pass, nor aught to certify,
That compensation had, in truth, been made,
By passage money, *bona fide* paid.
As frightened turtles in a panic slide
From sunny perch, in clumsy haste to hide;
So disappeared our doughty soldier boys,
As quick they heard the foe's approaching noise.
The search was made, and from each hiding place,
Was brought to light, full many a reckless face,

7

Whose guilt-stained features quietly revealed
What blust'ring words, and artful lips concealed.
Of muskets, too, a wagon load were seized,
Which latter feat, the marshal's ire appeased.
Then Parker French came driving down the pier,
With a crowd of patriots in the rear.

A rabble dense thus gathered round in strife,
In tumult rolled, a surging sea of life;
To which, each human face, an angry wave,
The frenzied tossing of the tempest gave.
'T was soon made known, that to the eager crowd,
But sixty-five tickets would be allowed.
This plain report, a savage howling drew;
Revolvers waved, and bitter curses flew.
Uplifted, all, their deadly weapons stay,
Ill-omened pause, that speaks a bloody fray.
But, softly speaks the wily agent, now,
And, brief explaining, quickly quells the row.

'Mid deaf'ning shouts, at last the steamer clears
Her anchorage, when, quick a sloop appears,
As from a distant wharf she glides away,
And swift pursues us o'er the tranquil bay.
Upon her deck appear, in spite of law,
Four hundred men for Nicaragua's war.
Our boat is checked; the other speeds anew,
While loudly jeer her desperado crew.
But now is heard, a deep, stentorian voice,
Whose well-known sound presents no other choice,
Than be detained, or from injunction fly;
For the tones we hear are the marshal's cry.

In yonder row-boat, lo! he swiftly nears,
Which high excites our worthy captain's fears.
So, leaving the marshal perched in his boat,
Loud screaming his order in clarion note;
Leaving the freebooters vainly to plead,
We paddle away with the utmost speed,

The Golden Gate his rocky bars displayed,
And San Francisco's hills farewell we bade.
Then, sailing by the far-famed passage way,
Dark orifice punctured by ocean's spry,
Bold giant rocks, 'mid frowning darkness piled
To dizzy height, o'erlook the surges wild.
Black sullen hills in mute defiance stand,
While far away, in gloomy silence grand,
'Mid murky clouds that dim the distant skies,
Long heavy chains of dismal mountains rise.
Deep yawning gulfs, and threat'ning gulches wide,
Ensconced in gloom, those barren wastes divide.

Of passengers, four hundred, all entire,
Full seventy-five there were, who did aspire
To wield the sword, and rifle, in a land
Where Cholera upheld his ghastly hand.
And when at morn, from mountain top upsprang
The tardy Sun, and joy through nature rang,
Two companies, of such as volunteered,
Were organized, and Col. Fry appeared,
With written charge, conferring high command
Of all recruits he might succeed to land,

Swift rolled the hours, as southward now we sailed,
For scenes of interest scarce ever failed.
The volunteers, by military drill,
Were taught to 'train the muscle to the will.'

In active service, weapons soon to bear,
They for the work did zealously prepare.
Though winds blew fierce, and billows high did heave,
The roll was called, each day at morn, and eve;
When, with his weapon, ev'ry volunteer,
For rifle drill, must at his post appear.

When three days out, one man was taken ill,
Refused all food, but brandy, drank, until
Two days from San Juan, when reason fled,
And wild fantasia seized his vacant head;
Then rushing to the deck by demon aid,
Without a word, one savage bound he made,
The guards to clear, but, one who chanced to stand
Beside the madman, quickly caught one hand.
His feet and hands were then securely bound,
Though by his yells the surging waves were drowned.
Then, dragged below, and laid upon the floor,
He plead, at first, then frantic, cursed and swore.
Now peals of horrid laughter filled the air,
Then some dire fancy drove him to despair.
" O shoot me, boys ! What ! hang a man for that !"
Then to his friends that close around him sat,
He fiercely said, with eyes that madly rolled,
" Treacherous knaves ! you 've sold my life for gold !"
Then quickly changed his frenzied look and tone.
As though the demon Lunacy had flown ;
And, gravely musing on his past misdeeds,
He tells them all, and for existence pleads.
" The money we spent for political use ;
But, hang a man for that ! O, dire abuse !"
Till midnight, near, incessant did he rave,
Then dying, soon beneath the rolling wave

His body sank, to find a peaceful sleep,
Or—feed the finny monsters of the deep.

The twelfth day came, and near the dead of night,
Juan del Sur rose on our gladdened sight.
Her gloom-set hills faint met our eager gaze,
As the chary moon shed feebly her rays.
When morning came, in boats we went ashore,
By passing through a hulk, not long before,
Called hospital; a pest-house, truer named,
For luckless fillibusters, sick, or maimed.

The town of San Juan, if fitly called,
Sits low at water's edge, by mountains walled,
Or lofty hills, beyond whose right extreme,
The Transit winds, and fertile meadows gleam.
Dense forest lands retire, and slowly rise,
Extending east, and north, where, 'mid the skies,
Of sunlit hue, volcanic mountains rear
Their smoky heads, 'mid clouds to disappear.
The little land-clasped bay, in hushed repose,
Untroubled lies, though fierce the tempest blows;
For, right and left, the noble hills extend
Their giant arms, its safety to defend.

By Spanish mules in clumsy coaches drawn,
While smooth the way, we rapid travelled on.
The volunteers at San Juan remained;
Though cause for which was not to us explained.
To Col. Fry, permission had been sent
To act at discretion.   Could aught prevent?
The sequel proved, excusable transgression,
He quick began to act without discretion.

Excusable, all, promptly did agree,
Sure, "breach of trust" ne'er had a better plea;
Compel the man to exercise discretion!
That useful gift was not in his possession!

Rough, mountain lands soon rose athwart our way,
And weary looks, the "*mulas*" did display.
Four puny brutes, half starved, but finely matched
In stubbornness, were to each coach attached.

A sailor-boy we found upon the way,
Who, as he said, was bound for Virgin Bay.
The Uncle Sam he'd left, the previous night,
With strong desire, in Walker's cause to fight.
A runaway, he'd taken care to hide,
And secretly his arms had been supplied.
But, ah! poor Jack, a sad, untimely fate
Stole o'er his path, and for his life laid wait.
Powder, and scouring sand, are not alike;
A service-rifle, not a marline spike.
To chide each act of carelessness, was vain;
His gun discharged—the ball passed through his brain.
So swift the missile's work,—no word he said;
No sound escaped his lips;—life instant fled.

The day was warm, but, breezes gently blew,
And graceful waved the palm-tree, and the yew.
Her thousand varied notes, glad nature sang,
In silent voice, that through our feelings rang.
Yet, discord sad, her echoed music made,
For, round each heart had fallen a dreary shade.
Bright smiling hills, on either side arise,
Yet, round their laughing summits, in disguise,

Fierce, hireling squads of base Chamorro's band,
To roll in squalid avalanche, might stand.
Sweet, spicy groves, and shady dells appear,
From whose recess, no wafted sound we hear,
Save the low chanting of the zephyr breeze,
Whose gentle touch draws music from the trees;
Yet, there might lurk a sanguinary foe,
Concealed in ambush, cat-like, crouching low.
By no means groundless, such surmises dire;
For there, in truth, the Serviles, two days prior,
A sad defeat had met, at Walker's hand,
And lost in combat ninety of their band.
Thence put to flight, they roamed the forest wide,
In petty squads, from sharp pursuit to hide.
Our guides had said, that naught could happen wrong,
As the Liberal cause was fixed, and strong.
That east, and west, across the Transit way,
They held a settled, undisputed sway.
Thus, lulled to sleep, all fear of coming harm,
Scarce any one had thought it best to arm.
Yet, now, full soon, we found sufficient cause,
To deem ourselves within a lion's claws.

'Mid noon-day's sun, and light's departing ray,
In silver beams stole o'er our lonesome way.
Bright joyous smiles that lit the liquid face
Of Nicaragua's lake, the Queen of Grace.
But, scattered thick around us did appear,
Sad records, mute, but eloquent and clear,
Of mortal woe; each tree a graven page;
Each foot of ground, a chronicle of rage.
A tale was told, that, ere the bloody fray,
Beside a tree where blackened embers lay,

A volunteer, fast bound by cruel gyve,
Base, Servile hands had tortured,—burned alive.

We entered, soon, the village Virgin Bay,
Where, on the lake, the boat La Virgin lay.

The little town beside the water lies,
And views the lake, upon whose bosom rise,
The Sister Mountains, lofty, side by side,
Like peerless queens, upon the waves to ride.

The signal bell soon calls us down the street,
To water's edge, the steamer's boat to meet;
And, soon upon La Virgin's deck we stand,
When each, in thought, perceives his native land,
Not far away, spread out before his gaze,
In tints of gold, illumed by fancy's rays.
But, ah! full many a heart now beating high
With joyous hope, is destined soon to lie
In death's embrace, in mould'ring slumber low,
In clods of earth, or 'neath the water's flow.
Why wait we here?   Sure all is ready now.
Why hugs the shore the boat's impatient prow?
Now, o'er the deck, a look we cast around,
That gave to vague suspicion, ample ground.
Six cannons grim, about her sides were wheeled,
All cleared her deck, as for a battle field.
Yet, "true," thought we, "the guns 'tis wise to take,
We may, perchance, meet cruisers on the lake."
A fillibuster sad, the steamer was,
And might be seized, with justifying cause;
Then, Servile knaves, who, stain of mercy lacked,
And scarce possessed discriminating tact,

Might chance to cut our throats, by some mistake,
Or, shoot us through the head, for pleasure's sake.

While restlessly, all moved in silence, dumb,
A cry we sudden heard, "The soldiers come!"
And, gazing backward o'er the Transit way,
Beheld them marching in the twilight gray.
They soon embarked, and joined us on the boat;
But, of their destination,—not a note.
The boat then moved upon her 'customed way,
With rapid stride, atoning for delay.

Upon the steamer's deck, we pass the night;
Yet, ere return the rays of morning light,
A shrill command, in startling tones addressed,
Pierces our ears, and breaks our quiet rest.
"Clear now the boat for action!" is the cry;
And, starting up, the doughty French, we spy.
All quick arise, to face a frowning foe,
Or danger dire, in what, they scarcely know;
Armada dread, or frowning Seventy-four,
In fancy see, and hear its deaf'ning roar.
But, lo! naught on the dim expanse appears,
The mystery to solve, or waken fears.
But, day-light soon dissolved the misty shade,
Night's cast-off robe, and quickly then displayed
San Carlos Fort, the San Juan beside,
Which river serves the flowing lake to guide.
No more could falsehood serve; so truth was told;
For Walker's service, clearly, we were sold.
"San Carlos Fort, the natives now possess.
Her frowning walls we may not pass, unless,

8

With us you join, and force her guns to yield.
We 've arms in store; if them you choose to wield
In self-defence, the fortress we can wrest,
And shoot the knaves who now her walls invest.
In self-defence, we say, in honest truth.
Pass on our way! yon savages, forsooth,
With rascal cannonade, would sink us low
On the wat'ry bed of the river's flow.
But, say you now, had we not compromised
A safe result, by purposes disguised,
And lawless company, against your will,
You 'd safe have passed, without a thought of ill.
You wide mistake this sanguinary foe.
Pass by their hostile battlements! No, no!
To seize these boats, the savages are bent.
Attempt to pass, and, speedily you 're sent,
To sleep with the pebbles beneath the lake;
The sleep of death, from which none ever wake.
You ask us now: 'Though this were truly so,
Was truth too true for passengers to know?'
The answer is: We acted for the best.
Submit the case to common reason's test.
Had all been told, their safety was not sure;
That, in their path, were dangers to endure,
Who, then, had left the wharf at Virgin Bay?
Fewer, by far, than who had wished to stay.
Yet. wherefore stay, with danger no less dire,
From Cholera, or skulking demon's fire?
Plain is the truth: as convoy we are come;
To guard your path upon the passage home.
So, join us, if you will, or yet, refuse;
You 're free to act; your province 'tis to choose.

Yet, mark you well: though we may act alone,
Your lives, with ours, must for defeat atone."
Though for occasion framed, this story seemed,
Some rays of truth, 'mid denser falsehood gleamed.
To aid their cause, the Liberals had seized
The Transit boats, whene'er their fancy pleased.
'T was not for ours. but for the boat's protection,
They 'd dogged our steps, and formed this ill connection.
Yet, true it was, though danger lurked ahead,
At Virgin Bay, lay dangers no less dread.

A question now was promptly to be met,
With fruitful possibilities beset.
Contingencies, teeming with good or ill;
With seeming choice, yet necessary, still.
Upon the boat, as she to battle goes,
Must we lie still, while life's red current flows?
Beneath the deck, pale, helpless women lie;
Shall we supinely lay us down to die?
To take the proffered arms, we gave consent,
With scarce a voice to utter discontent.
Grave was the step, for, fillibusters, now,
To outlaws' fate, if luckless, we must bow.

Upon a hill, beside the river's source,
San Carlos stood, to guard its winding course;
And, save this hill, with one upon its right,
No landing-place there broke upon our sight.
For, all beside is low and marshy ground,
With thicket dense, and dismal jungle bound.
Both little hills rise on the river's left,
Like orphans lone, from all their kindred reft.

To cannon's range, we neared the fortress hill,
When, in a boat, though quite against his will,
Our steamer's captain carried to the land,
A formal charge the fortress to demand.
The shore he reached, but came not back again.
Reply to give, the natives did not deign.
Quick to and fro their dusky gunners flew,
Then o'er the lake a cannon-shot they threw.
A thirty-two, the missile seemed to be,—
Naught heavier than eighteen pounds, had we.
So, quick 'twas thought more prudent to retire,
Than madly stay, and brave their rascal fire.
Our quiet call they haughtily had spurned,
And speedily the compliment returned.

As now we moved, their deadly guns to clear,
Another ball, well aimed, came bounding near.
With giant stride, in threat'ning haste it came,
But, haply fell, to sink beside its game.
With feelings, mixed, of pleasure, and of fear,
We gazed to see each cannon's smoke appear.
First, columns dense of silent vapor flow,
When, bursting forth, red fiery volumes glow,
And, 'mid the flame, out leaps the angry ball
From cannon's mouth, upon the waves to fall.
From thence repelled, a frightful bound it makes,
Descends again, again a curvet takes.
The tardy sound then ambles on apace,
Outstrips the ball, and easy wins the race.

Now bearing left, to clear the fortress guns,
Our heedless boat, athwart new danger runs.

Yon wood-crowned height, San Carlos' sister hill,
All quiet lay, deceitfully, until
Her range we neared, when, guns before concealed,
Sprang into view, and belching music pealed.
But, ' haste made waste ;' her balls, correctly aimed
Their mark to strike, were by the waters tamed.

Of passengers, but few were now averse
A fight to join, but willing to amerce
A recompense for jeopardy in strife,
By mulct assessed in currency of life.
Yet, some there were, of apprehensive mind,
Who murmured low, to fate but ill resigned.
One cautious man, when urged to join the scheme,
With timid face lit up in hopeful gleam,
In anxious tone proceeded to inquire :
"Will they shoot back when we begin to fire ?"
"O, certainly ! they'll pay us back our coin."
" Ah ! well," he gravely said, " then I shan't join."
So ludicrous, the colloquy thus held,
All rueful thought was instantly dispelled.
Loud peals of laughter broke from all around,
And left each mind an echo of their sound.

Intent to gain possession of the hill,
Full forty men, in boats, with ready will,
With rifles and revolvers, fitly armed,
Now left the steamer's side, which quick alarmed
The garrison who held San Carlos height.
And down they came, our volunteers to fight.
This sudden move was not to our desire ;
So, bearing down, in haste, we opened fire

Upon the fort, to draw her men again.
But, all our guns were brought to bear in vain;
For, when discharged, their balls flew not away,
The fort to scathe, but, to our great dismay,
Upon the waves fell quick to disappear,
When loud we heard the native wretches jeer.

Their force entire, three hundred men, or more,
In grim array, now lined a hostile shore.
The boats, midway, were boldly pushing on,
While toward the fort, discharging guns anon,
Our steamer swiftly pressed, all hands alert,
Some quite alarmed, but no one badly hurt.
One Irishman who moodily sat by,
Thus to his thoughts gave language with a sigh:
"Ah! soon will blaze their cannon's red'ning glow,
Then, sure ye'll see the blood begin to flow."
With downcast look, another paced the deck
Like a storm-bound mariner doomed to wreck.
"Alas!" said he, "my wife, and children wait
For him whose steps are turned aside by fate.
With anxious gaze the mother looks, in vain,
For him whose face she ne'er shall see again.
My children dear, trip lightly as the fawn,
In hope to meet their father o'er the lawn.
But ah! they turn, with saddened faces, home,
To shroud a mother's heart in deeper gloom.
Dread poverty a widow's cup shall fill;
The fatherless must drain the dregs of ill."
Deep now is heard the distant tempest's sigh,
And, suddenly, dark clouds o'erspread the sky.
For full an hour the angry tempest roars,
The billows toss, a blinding torrent pours.

No boats nor shore, no natives now appear;
By gloom obscured, no frowning ramparts rear.
The boat is checked; but, elements enraged,
Our foe have joined, and in the strife engaged.
Aghast we stand, beneath the tempest's pow'r,
Whose watr'y jaws now threaten to devour
Our absent boats; but, soon old Nature flies;
Withdraws her forces, bids her legions rise;
And distant, then, approaching from the lee,
The missing ones, our bold recruits we see,
As, wearily and slow, they drag along,
With sinking boats, and faces woe-begone.
Ere they could touch upon that hostile land,
The storm had poured upon their little band;
When quick o'erwhelmed amid the falling tide,
'T was vain to move, for, naught their way could guide.

Another consultation now is held,
Which quick decides, by circumstance compelled,
The scheme to drop, and sail without delay,
Across the lake, again, to Virgin Bay.
'T was not for lack of fortitude possessed,
The plan had failed San Carlos to invest;
For, braver men than formed that lawless crew,
The wildest page of story never knew.
Our cannon-balls had proved to be too small;
This fact explained their very speedy fall.
Another truth lay not at all concealed:
The steamer's hull quite easily would yield
To cannon-shot, for, made of iron thin,
Her strength would fail, and let the missiles in.
Then woe to us, should some unlucky shot,
On evil bent, pierce through the boilers hot.

The women, too, their faces blanched with fright,
Imploringly had said, " O, do not fight!"

Bold French and Fry, now brilliant speeches made,
Quite plausible, with arguments arrayed,
To prove their course a philanthrophic plan
To elevate a lower race of man.
This lofty aim had moved their noble feet
From peaceful homes, and caused their hearts to beat
In kindly sympathy; their souls inspired
With high resolve, and noble impulse, fired.
Like La Fayette, they'd nobly volunteered
For liberty, where tyrants domineered.
A glorious few, devoted to the cause
Of snatching men from foul Oppression's claws.
So free their hearts from ev'ry thought of guile,
Angelic hosts might well look down, and smile.
Naught else but good, had brought this precious band
From happy homes, to roam a foreign land.

The sun was low; 't was near the close of day,
When o'er the lake we sailed, for Virgin Bay.
There, with the dead of night, to get ashore,
All crowded out, and thought of nothing more,
Till, gazing back upon the moonlit bay,
We saw our convoy sailing fast away.
Thus left were we, defenceless and alone,
Our Great-Hearts gone, our kind protectors flown.

The night passed on, and day began to break,
When, dim in distance o'er the placid lake,
A boat appeared, fast heading into port,
Apparently from old San Carlos fort.

All eyes were turned with scrutinizing gaze,
And, in some bosoms, hope began to raise.
The stranger boat arrived, and proved to be
San Carlos, named, which filled us full of glee.
Now these had passed the fortress walls secure,
That we might safely pass, seemed likewise sure.
But, very brief such happiness, for, lo!
They quickly told a dismal tale of woe:
With noontide's sun upon the previous day,
While off the fort, we in La Virgin lay,
The boat, San Carlos, braved the San Juan,
As, slow and sure against the tide she ran.
Unconscious, quite, of all that had occurred,
They passed the fort, when quick commanding word
The natives gave, and gruffly bade them stay.
This, lucklessly, they dared to disobey,
When instant belched an angry thirty-two,
Whose deadly missile pierced the steamer through.
From cannon's mouth a quick descent it made,
But rose again in added strength arrayed,
Passed through the boat as through a paper toy;
Two lives destroyed, and maimed a little boy.
The boat was stopped; a native posse came,
Expecting there to find exquisite game.
But, high and low, in vain a search was made;
She carried naught for fillibuster aid.
So, quietly the searching troop withdrew,
And left the boat her journey to pursue.

Full sad the tale of those who suffered there,
A wife and mother, with her children fair.

9

A lovely girl whose age five summers told,
A little boy, then scarcely six years old.
They'd left their home, the far off west to greet,
The husband and the father, there to meet.
Within her berth the happy mother lay,
While by her side the children were at play;
But, swiftly on its direful mission came
The cannon ball, and, such its deadly aim,
From larboard bow, it pierced the upper deck,
Of all that interposed made instant wreck;
Passed through the berth wherein the mother lay,
Her life destroyed,—tore limb from limb away;
The daughter slew, and pilfered, as it left,
The boy's right foot,—sad, sanguinary theft!
Still resistless, on it madly went,
Till, far away upon the lake it spent.
With strangers, now, all friendless and alone,
The wounded boy was left to wail and moan;
But, on a litter, carried o'er the way,
He lived to enter San Francisco Bay.

California passengers passed on,
And we were left, our fate to muse upon.
'T was ascertained, that, very close at hand,
Nine miles away, at Rivas, was a band,
Eight hundred strong, of Chamorrista braves,
Who, well we knew, would gladly dig our graves.
More willingly, if yet by chance they knew
That we so late had joined a hostile crew.

Some now desired San Carlos boat to take,
And once again, cross eastward o'er the lake.

But others said, " 'T were folly thus to go
Athwart their path, so wittingly to throw
Our lives away, or poise them in the scale,
With native mercy, hoping to prevail."

The day passed on; low in the west, the sun
All cloudless sank, his race of glory run.
In anxious groups, the passengers conversed,
Their hopes and fears, their future plans rehearsed;
While 'neath the roof by company possessed,
Were gathering, full many, there to rest.
The house was low; damp earth its only floor;
One story high, and through each end a door.
A stairway rose, within, upon the right,
Ascending to its second-story height,
Another pile, the company's estate,
In which, below, were vehicles and freight.
Around the rear, a spacious yard was laid,
Three sides enclosed by fence, or palisade.

Old Night came on; her deep'ning shadows fell
In rayless gloom, that blackened hill, and dell.
The stars shone not, nor Luna gave her light;
Dark, threat'ning clouds enhanced the gloom of night.
All hushed was nature's voice; the air was calm,
Though softly waved the gentle zephyr's arm.
Some passengers were roaming through the town,
And many more, outside, were sitting down.
But greater, still, the number gathered in
Beneath the lower roof, with busy din,
Preparing for the night; some lying down,
Invoking sleep, solicitude to drown;

While scatt'ring groups in moody silence stood,
Or low conversed, to augur ill, or good.
The feeble rays of churlish tapers dim,
Came straggling forth, from murky lanterns, grim,
When, lo ! a sound of tramping, and a yell,—
A hideous sound, as from a demon, fell.
Then followed, quick, a shout of savage glee,
As from a host of prisoned imps set free,—
The doorway swarmed with savage musketeers,
And deaf'ning sounds of weapons filled our ears;
When, 'mid the smoke and fire, poured in a show'r
Of musket balls, with swift and fatal pow'r,—
Deep groans of pain, with accents of despair,
Commingled, all, rose on the midnight air.
One man, engaged in conversation low,
Close by my side, deep groaned in mortal woe,—
Fell prostrate on that humid, earthy floor,
With ghastly wound, to welter in his gore.
No tongue can tell, no pen can e'er portray
That scene of death, of horror and dismay.
The sleepers rose in terror from the ground,
From dreams of woe, to see their visions crowned.
Many who rose, back quickly fell again,
To print the earth with many a crimson stain.
Low on the ground, myself in haste I threw,
While thick around, the whizzing bullets flew;
But, to and fro, the mass in frenzy rolled,
And quick increased their shrieks of woe, ten fold;
For, in the rear, from whence they sought to go,
Again they met the sanguinary foe,
Who drove them back, with yells of fierce delight;
Then, up the stairs they took a hasty flight.

Meanwhile, without, o'er savage howls arose
The cries of men, pursued by bloody foes.
Defenceless, all, life worthless seemed, and lost;
And hope was vain, to sell them at a cost.
While prostrate, there, upon the ground I lay,
All motionless, and cold as passive clay,
Swift-moving Thought had travelled far and wide,
Passed land and sea, with one prodigious stride,
O'erlooked the scenes of childhood's happy hours,
Roamed o'er the hills, and culled the wildwood flowers.
Then, O, the pang, when back she came again,
And sadly said, " Resign all hope, as vain !
Though hard the fate, inhale thy latest breath,
For, lo ! beside thee stands the monster Death."

Incessant flowed a stream of lead and fire;
The bullets sped, and crashed, with fearful ire.
Above, below, pierced ev'ry side around,
And baggage all, piled high upon the ground.
But, soon was spent the fury of attack;
The knaves had found material for sack.
Then quick upsprang, who like myself had lain,
Low on the ground, all breathless as the slain,
Three passengers, and ran with nimble pace,
To join the crowd within their refuge place;
And to their flight, my own was added soon,
With eager step, to gain protection's boon.
'Mid random fire, the loft we gained, unharmed,
When, lo ! a sight that feeble hope alarmed.
Pale, deathlike men we saw assembled there,
Like marble statues, lit by candles' glare.
Cold, glassy eyes from rigid features gazed,
And on each head the quiv'ring hair upraised.

Still, others moved, with silent, ghost-like tread,
Believing scarce that life had not yet fled;
And many more, with groans of pain and woe,
There sought to staunch the crimson current's flow,
From ghastly wounds, that yet profusely bled,
Smearing them o'er with blood, from foot to head.
None hoped for life; each face spoke blank despair;
Death seemed to claim a kindred with the air.
But timid Thought, though first to fly away,
Had rallied soon to claim her house of clay.
Grim savages, we knew our foes to be,
Yet, pris'ners close, 't were vain, the hope to flee.
Of all our band, but two, alone, possessed
Defensive means, yet, well they bore the test
Of courage true; for, powder none had they,
Save what within their trusty weapons lay.
Revolvers drawn, by firmness doubly manned,
They by the staircase boldly took a stand,
Resolved to die, defending to the last,
Their lives, and manhood, menaced by the blast
That fiercely howled, with life-destroying sound,
And close beset their prison walls around.
No savages had yet in sight appeared,
But, far more dread a danger now we feared.
'T would well become their sanguinary fame,
To fire the house, and shoot us through the flame.

A company, myself with other two,
Now searched, in hope to break our prison through.
With silent step, two rooms were quickly passed,
As on each side a searching glance was cast,
For avenues that might perchance be near,
To penetrate the building to its rear.

A narrow way at last we chanced to spy,
That outward led upon a balcon high,
On which went out, myself, and one beside,
Resolved to flee, or, failure to abide.
Without the door, in silent pace we stepped,
As stealthily, on hands and knees, then crept.
Across the building's rear, from side to side,
The balcony was laid, but not supplied,
As soon we found, with stairway to descend,
Nor colonnade, with friendly posts to lend.

With human woe, still rang the ev'ning air,
Some begging life, some wailing in despair,
While tramp of horse, and rider's brutal cry,
With discord dire, resounded in reply.
With wary eye, around the balcon's right
A glance we cast, when saw a fearful sight,—
In close pursuit, a band of natives ran,
With passengers swift flying in the van.
Another squad had gathered close around
A murdered man, there stretched upon the ground;
And o'er the corse, those grim assassins fought,
To share the gold their bloody knives had bought.
Now peering o'er the balcon's railing low,
With deep dismay, within the yard below,
A sentinel we saw, there placed on guard,
To intercept all passing through the yard.
But, happily, thick clouds were o'er the sky,
And through their gloom he had not chanced to spy
Our lurking-place, for, while reflected light
His post revealed, it dimmed his clearer sight.

Beyond one side, and round the building's end,
A passage-way did to the street extend;
Where window lights their bright reflection made,
The passage lit, threw us in deeper shade.
No word we spoke, but silent groped our way;
No sound was made that might our lives betray.
The ground below, in distance twenty feet,
Quick might we reach, but, jumping, death must meet.
We might, perchance, alight in safety there,
Yet, with the guard not quite so easy fare.
The balcony we quickly crossed again,
With trembling hopes that fast began to wane,
When looking o'er the railing at the side,
Below the balcony, a brace we spied.
Companion, first, the rail sprang lightly o'er,
And, quick ensconced beneath the structure's floor,
An effort made, the yard below to gain,
But, soon returning, called the project vain.
Then, scarce in hope for fortune's better aid,
The brace I gained; the same attempt then made.
Suspended now, full fifteen feet in air,
I thought to drop; on what, knew not, nor where,
When, scarce two feet below, upon the right,
The lower roof appeared, a welcome sight.
A sudden swing the object then obtained,
A noiseless fall,—the tile-laid roof was gained.
Now looking back, to bid my comrade haste,
No one appeared, and moments must not waste;
For time was life, and death might crown delay.
This prudent thought forbade me longer stay.

Night's sable hue had deepened with her hours,
And airy hosts were marshalling their pow'rs.

Old Darkness, soon, his deepest robe had flung
O'er nature's lovely form, and silent hung
His blackest drapery o'er hill and dale,
O'er mountain top, and through the lonely vale.
Full dire the thought, as down the roof I crept,
That now, perchance, destruction only slept
Coiled serpent-like, and prone upon my path,
Full soon to wake, and spend his venom wrath.

A dark abyss now met my eager gaze,
And straining eyes were vain to pierce the maze.
A moment's pause,—then springing through the gloom
For aught apparent, hasting on to doom,
By fortune's aid I safely reached the ground,
When, casting quick a searching glance around,
Beheld a sight that chilled my blood with fear.
Within the doorway at the building's rear,
Another guard, a brawny savage paced,
While 'neath the roof a gang were laying waste
The baggage, all, with freedom uncontrolled,
With clumsy haste, in greedy search for gold.
Yet undiscovered, hastily I ran,
With scarce the thought a proper course to plan,
And, fortunately, gained the palisade,
But found it quite too high for escalade.
Quick turning, then with feelings of dismay,
And fearful lest, my purpose to betray,
With passive treachery the very air
Should to the foe each silent footstep bear,
With fearful haste an aperture I sought,
Hope sinking fast, each step with danger fraught.
Yet now appeared, when heart began to fail,
An open space where lay a broken pale.

10

This passing through, I gained the woodland near,
Nor had the thought, escape might prove too dear.

With shouts of natives, still the forest rang,
Pursuers, all, in many a petty gang;
While heavy clouds began to cast their store;
With open hands their ill-timed gifts to pour.
Long 'mid the rain, there, in that forest wide,
Alone, I sought from sharp pursuit to hide.
Loud voices raised, a friendly tone to feign:
" All's right, now, boys! come back to town again!"
But, Spanish accent boded not of good:
'T was plain a ruse to draw us from the wood.
Wandering round, a voice at last I heard,
In whispered tone, that spoke a magic word:
" American are you?" it softly said,
In accent fraught with mingled hope, and dread.

Rejoiced to note a friendly voice so near,
And speaking low that foemen might not hear,
I nearer drew, the whispered tones my guide,
When, lo! there sat together side by side,
Three passengers close round a dwarfish tree,
Half dead with fright, who gladly welcomed me.
Each had a tale full marvelous to tell,
And all agreed, 't was luck to fare so well.
Soon from a tree-top down came other two,
And joined our little band, which rapid grew,
Till, ere an hour, it numbered twelve, in all,
Of ev'ry age, of sizes, great and small.

We now discussed, an action to pursue,
But each had plans, and projects, not a few.

Each thought his own had quite the brightest look;
So, long we argued ere an action took.
" To San Juan," some said, " T is best to go,"
But to this project others answered: " No !
For, on the way quite sure are we to find
Each road-side hedge with straggling natives lined.
'T is wiser, far, here in the wood to stay,
And lay our plans by clearer light of day."

The night was warm, but fast the chilling rain
Cold o'er us fell, to make our danger twain;
For Cholera had stretched his ghastly hand,
To sweep and scourge with death that fairy land.
And ev'ry blast must serve to haste his sway,
Each drop of rain, to pave his cruel way.

'T was midnight near; all sound had died away,
When there, at last, all did agree to stay.
Then searching round for shelter from the blast,
A tree we found with spreading branches vast,
Around whose trunk all soon lay fast asleep,
Save one, who offered watchman's post to keep.
But swarming ants soon added to our woes,
And, creeping o'er us, broke our short repose.
Then, ere in sleep again our cares were drowned,
From o'er the lake a cannon's booming sound,
In volume clear, was wafted on the breeze,
And echoed loud by giant forest trees.
This, on our minds the quick impression made,
That Walker's band had come to give us aid.
But all was hushed in deep repose again,
And on we slept, till darkness closed his reign.
Then rising, all, were quite surprised to see
Two passengers descending from a tree,

Within whose top they'd spent a weary night,
Nor dared to leave, from sheer excess of fright.
Yet, one was armed, and now with valor true,
A small revolver from his pocket, drew.

'T' was soon resolved to send a party out,
To bring report if Serviles were about.
To reconnoitre with a watchful eye,
To learn their force, and every movement spy.
Three of the band were chosen for the scout,
And, on the venture, quickly we set out;
First marking well our comrade's lurking place,
That, easily, our steps we might retrace.
One comrade was a New York doctor, old,
Who, long before, had left his craft for gold.
Many a year of wand'ring he had passed,
'T' was thus his story ran, till now, at last,
As age came on, too old to wander more,
With wisdom gained, he sought his native shore.
The other was a man of stalwart frame,
Pike-County boy, of California fame,

We travelled on, with caution but with speed,
The doctor claiming, as his right, the lead.
Leaving the paths a denser way to take,
We soon espied, with joy, the placid lake;
But, sound of native voices quickly heard,
And, lying low, spoke not a whispered word;
When soon appeared a company, which, lo!
Though native, all, was not a savage foe.
A band of women, they, with downcast look,
Who, for their lives, thus pleasant homes forsook.
Deep in the wood, a drear abode they sought,
A houseless home, with death and danger fraught.

Their cruel kindred no distinction made,
Between their foes, and such as gave them aid.
Sons, husbands, fathers, brothers, had espoused
The hostile cause, by which had been aroused
That deadly hate which none but Spaniards feel,
And which had pledged the oath that death must seal.
When told our mission, where we thought to go,
Their heads they shook, and sorrowful, said " No !"
"Your lives," said they, "must pay the forfeit dear,
Should, on your way, a Servile band appear."
But, marching on, all soon drew near the lake,
Along whose shore, a course we thought to take.
A point of land, dense wooded, lay between,
Which, from our view the village served to screen.
But, off the town, upon the tranquil bay,
The Transit boat San Carlos, quiet lay.
Then knew we well, the cannon that had woke
From sleep, the midnight air, her coming spoke.
But whence she came, and what her motives were,
We nothing knew, and little could infer.
Yet, this was known : upon the previous day,
Ere noontide came, she'd swiftly sped away.
No object moved upon her tranquil deck ;
All, silent seemed, deserted as a wreck.
"Yet," thought we now, "assistance may be near,
While we like reptiles, crouch, and creep in fear."
Defenceless, true, and wishing were to trifle,
As wishes, all, could not produce one rifle.

The clouds of night had with her passed away,
And brightly smiled the rising orb of day.
And gently waved upon the morning breeze,
The rain-clad foliage of the trees.

The lake we left, and tracked the forest through,
The road to seek, and gain a fairer view.
And from a point upon the Transit way,
We soon beheld the village, and the bay.
But, naught to fear was there, our eyes to greet;
No Servile soldiers marched the quiet street.
All sound was hushed; but, measuredly, and slow
Were human beings, moving to and fro,
Yet, friends, or foes, our eyes could not discern,
And the doctor said, " 'T is wise to return."
So, when was moved a venture into town,
He sagely looked, and answered with a frown:
" Let age's counsel be the guide of youth,
In times of danger as in ways of truth.
Imprudent rashness, wisdom does abhor.
'There's art in council, policy in war.'"
Our feet we turned, a pathless way to trace,
When prompted Thought, perhaps with ill-born grace:
"The old man's prudence speaks his inward fears,
And not the gain of 'multitude of years.'"
His maxims wise, with such discernment fraught,
Were learned of fear, and not by wisdom taught.

Now to the ambush where our comrades lay,
Direct we thought to go, but lost the way;
And long there sought amid the forest wide,
With naught that served our wayward feet to guide,
Till when, at last, we chanced to wander back
Upon the road, and took our morning track.
Then quick retraced, the journey of the morn,
We joined our comrades, who, of hope forlorn,
Despairing, quite, our safe return to see,
Loud welcomed us with more than childish glee.

Like famished wolves they ate in greedy haste,
The food we brought, and there before them placed.
'T was wheaten cake, and bread of maize, or corn,
Of native women purchased in the morn.

Our counsel-board was ruled by caution's voice,
To enter town was not our comrades' choice.
But soon, in mass, returning to the lake,
Our scouting band a new excursion make.
Though wearily, in hopeful spirit strong,
We cautious moved, the water's edge along,
And on the shore, in distance, soon espied,
Three Spanish girls, who, walking side by side,
With hasting step, seemed eagerly intent,
On purpose high, on some grave mission bent.
Though first unseen, our party soon they spied,
And, running toward us, eagerly they cried,
"No Chamorro! No Walker! No combat!
"No pistol, gun! No bang! No mas combat!"
With noble features, lit by sparkling eyes,
Whose beaming spoke kind hearts to sympathize,
And faces, all, with glad excitement flushed,
Their words, as from a fount, in torrent gushed.
The Servile band had left at break of day,
Three hundred men, weighed down with spoil, and prey.
Of passengers, close held the previous night,
As prisoners within the building's height,
None suffered harm who scathless there remained,
When, from the party my escape was gained;
For, to the band the Transit's agent spoke,
Their cause to plead, and mercy to invoke.
The party's chief, a Frenchman chanced to be,
Who soon, humanely, set the captives free.

To seek the town, we left without delay,
Our fair companions, pilots of the way.
Six men had died; four in the room below,
And two outside who'd thought to brave the foe.
Fifteen were wounded, groaning in their woe
Some slightly harmed, others by mortal blow;
And though appeared no more who suffered wound,
One hundred and fifty could not be found.

Grenada city, anxious now to see,
A plan was formed, though all did not agree,
San Carlos boat, to take, without delay,
And seek that town, full eighty miles away.
There Walker was, and there, "forsooth," thought we,
"Our nation's legate we shall doubtless see."
The bay we left, and with the eve drew near
An island, lone, where "Sister Mountains" rear.
There took in wood; until the morning lay,
Then sailed again, direct for Virgin Bay.
Upon the pier was many a hopeful face,
Whose struggling joy concealed affliction's trace.
Full twenty-five of missing ones we found,
Then sailed again, for old Grenada bound.
Passed Ometepee near close of the day,
And in the morning, off the city lay,
As sailors said, but, intervening wood
Concealed the height on which the city stood.
Beside the water's margin, stood a fort,
Though much decayed, still used to guard the port;
Yet vainly used, for, distant left or right,
No barrier rose to check a foeman's might.
Upon the lake-shore horsemen soon appeared,
Republicans, we hoped, yet Scrviles, feared.

The stars and stripes waved o'er that ancient fort,
Yet, held by Serviles, well it would comport
With native strategy, and impulse low,
To hang false colors out, to trap a foe.

The agent, Scott, conductor on the lake,
Though hesitating, soon agreed to take
An embassy, intent to ascertain
If landing, now, were added loss or gain.
But, Liberals, the horsemen proved to be,
And on the boat, 't was soon our joy to see
Our nation's envoy; Wheeler was his name,
And many thought he played a double game.
To us, his counsel was, to land and stay
Till Walker's arms should force the Transit way.
"Within the bounds of old Grenada's wall,
You 're safe," said he, "whatever may befall;
For Walker, now, is well established there;
And all expense our government will bear."

Around the town was built a massive wall,
Impregnable, with iron portals tall,
Which opened wide our party to invite,
Then, crashing, closed, like giants in their might.
Narrow the streets, and by a novel plan,
Into a plaza, all, converging, ran;
And on this plaza, seeming in parade,
Brave Walker's force entire were now arrayed.
Yet, soon we learned, more serious work had they,
Than marching round, their weapons to display.
An enemy, hard by the northern gate,
One thousand strong, for blood insatiate,
In hurried march, now threatened an assault,
Which possibly might bring an ill result.
11

Each avenue was strongly fortified,
While nimbly spurring o'er from side to side,
Bold William moved, among his fearless band,
Quick speaking words of counsel, or command.
At medium height, the dauntless William stood,
A hero, scarce, nor yet a Robin Hood.
Beneath a Panama, his piercing eyes
Bespoke a man, if not a statesman wise,
Of active mind, in stubborn purpose great,
Whose spirit proud, no master knew, save fate.
A chair was standing on the plaza's side,
In which, e'en now, the bold Salitzer died.
A prisoner, with freedom, on parole,
A correspondence with the foe he'd stole.
Compell'd to sit upon that chair of death,—
Full twenty bullets stole away his breath.
As we approached, they bore his sad remains,
Leaving the chair smeared o'er with blood and brains.

The evening came, and as no stir was made
In Servile camp, to sleep we soon essayed.
But in the night loud cannon roars were heard,
And those who wakened easily inferred
A night attack, with murd'rous cannonade,
And, yet defenceless, all were quite dismayed.
But, creeping out with nervous step, some learned
What into joy their apprehensions turned.
Within the night proposals had been sent,
Which quickly served a battle to prevent.
To yield their arms, the Serviles had agreed,
And to the rule of Liberals concede,
If to their faction wealth should be restored,
And former lines of party be ignored.

At ten o'clock, to lay their weapons down,
Without the walls, and quiet enter town.
But, knowing well the nature of their foe,
And doubting, still, that danger would not flow,
To be prepared, the Liberals resolved,
For peace or war, till time all doubt had solved.

The passengers, by Wheeler's counsel swayed,
Now organized to volunteer their aid,
In case the knaves in treachery were fain,
By stratagem the city's walls to gain
With arms concealed.   But, to their promise true,
At ten o'clock, they to the city drew.
The chieftains met; each, friendly glances cast;
In Spanish tongue, congratulations passed.
On noble steeds, the Serviles moved with grace,
And stood their hardy foemen, face to face.
But now came news from old San Carlos hill,
Which caused us quick to travel with a will.
The garrison who held that lonely height,
For cause unknown, had taken hasty flight.
So in one hour, passed through the city's gate,
Our party all, save who, controlled by fate,
In death's embrace, or fell disease's pow'r,
Lay helpless, low, to wait a dying hour.
At Ometepec, again with night we staid.
And at return of day, our anchor weighed;
Made Virgin Bay long ere the daylight's wane,
In hope some news of missing ones to gain.
Nor vain the hope, for on the lake's green shore,
Of old companions, forty-five, or more,
In sight appeared, who since the bloody fray,
Had ventured not their presence to display.

When first in view our well-known steamer hove,
The wood they left, and hastened to the cove.
Then soon, upon the steamer stood unharmed,
From woe relieved, and apprehensions calmed.

The town we left, and found at Carlos hill,
La Virgin's captain, who, against his will,
Had been detained since o'er the fortress wall,
He boldly stepped, to speak our modest call.
Deserted now, and silent was the height,
No cannons frowned, as conscious of their might.
But dire disease soon trod a crimson path
Through human life, with more than mortal wrath.
Full seventy men we'd left at Virgin Bay,
And twenty more the scourge soon stole away.

As day bequeathed dominion to the night,
The moonlit air revealed Castillo height,
Where landing, all, we passed the Rapids' flow,
Took smaller boats, and quickly on did go.
Our hopes at morn were deep with danger fraught,
In fog obscured, near San Juan del Norte.
This vapor dense, though scattered by the light,
Still served to hide Mosquetia's coast from sight.
"Star of the West" in waiting here we found,
And in her left, for New York Harbor bound.
Passed Cuba's west, by Gulf of Mexico,
Then bearing northward, tracked the Gulf Stream's flow.
November third, we entered New York Bay,
And, safe at last, in Hudson River lay,
As all confessed, with fortunes scanty doled;
Experience in greater store than gold.

www.ingramcontent.com/pod-product-compliance
Lightning Source LLC
Chambersburg PA
CBHW032352020726
47499CB00008B/2711